The Rising Sun and other Sun stories

by Carys Smith

Contents

Proofread: Eileen Harries
Editors: Graham & Carol Whitaker
Front Cover Imagery: Thomas Williams
Back Cover Imagery: David Walker
Publishing: Artbully, UK

*All three short story volumes are
dedicated to Enfys Jones*

Bitter truth and Sweet sunshine:

Truth is bitter, the bitter
the better.

Truth tastes bitter on tongues that
hate truth.

Truth is like transparent glass or
a golden fish without a place
to hide.

Truth may be hidden for quite a
while in darkness.

Truth is the end of darkness.

Truth should surpass all else.

Be ready to speak truth or do not
speak.

Truths are sweet words of sunshine.

Footnote: (poem co-written by Dele Apeji and Carys Smith)

Dele Apeji posted a version of this poem on The Poetry Wall. I was struck by the imagery and the passionate cry for Truth – even" bitter truth." Through collaboration via social media, we worked together to create an English translation. I am merely the amanuensis; the translator; the shaper into poetic form.

As a political activist Dele has held onto one dream for many years: a united Nigeria where all are free to speak Truth. A time to come when Nigeria no longer sits on a" keg of gunpowder"; a time when Truth surpasses all else; a time when Truths are sweet words of sunshine.

Civvy. Street:
April 1947
Mr. Cyril Atkinson

"Father will get me a decent suit," decided Cyril. This was just an exchange of one uniform for another. He folded the extra shirts and underwear into the flimsy suitcase, shoving the felt cap and tie into its corner. He studied his discarded army fatigues for a moment then hung them with the unclaimed empty jackets. They made him think of all the unreturned dead; his mates left in Belgium and Germany; those poor buggers in the camps. They would never need another change of clothes. He turned away quickly forcing his mind back to his new civvy suit and his first day of freedom.

The grey pinstripe was a bit on the short side but so was the brown and the blue. The trousers looked like they were having an argument with his shoes. The cloth was good though: Burtons. Beatie or Betty or mother could make something from the material. He wanted a proper suit now he was back in Civvy Street: one which said Mr Atkinson not Corporal Atkinson.

He left the Regents Park Barracks without a backward glance and turned down Albany Street for the Tube. He tried to remember not to swing his arms and fling his left leg forward but could not stop his whistling. It had become as much a part of him as the khaki he had just left behind. He began "Pack up your Troubles." He was proud of the rare musicality of his whistle. It had helped his troop march the bloodstained, mud-clogged, or dusty miles from France to Germany. They had called him The Merry Whistler. These days, although he did not realise it, there was a melancholy undertone that accompanied even the catchiest of his tunes. He slowed to a deliberate stroll stopping at a kiosk to buy more tobacco, a paper and as an afterthought, a bunch of primroses from the woman in front of the station.

From the tube he walked across to Canon Street and waited for the train to Dartford. It was full of other demobbed men in identical suits, all weather hardened like himself, breathing in Blighty's smokey air of freedom.

"Coming for a pint Corp?" It was Sid Tunbridge. He gave Cyril a big gap-toothed grin. He had lost most of his top teeth in a bar fight but always said they had been "blown clean out" by a grenade in Antwerp. Sid liked to talk about the war. He had already turned it into a Boy's Own adventure. Cyril hesitated. Beatie would be expecting him by six but a quick stop for a pint at the Orange Tree would do no harm.

"I'm Cyril from now on Sid," he said, "Just plain old Cyril or I'll tell all the ladies how you really lost your teeth."

Cyril only intended the one pint but there were too many people wanting to buy him a beer; a darts match he was bound to win and a pretty barmaid with dark bold eyes and too much lipstick above a mustard- coloured scarf. After the third pint he bought her a gin and lime, presented her with the wilted flowers then sat down to a game of Pontoon.

The dream of a quiet clean house and a bit of garden had been the one thing that had kept him going through his war but now, as he sat with his mates in the loud fuggy bar, he felt like he was home already: a room crowded with men like himself; men with a shared hideous knowledge and a secret language only they understood.

"Goodbye Corporal Atkinson," he said leaning into the bar as if it might fall down, "free at last." He raised a glass to his grainy reflection, blew a kiss to the barmaid and left the pub to start on his last march into Civvy Street.

But as he began the walk, three hours late and not quite sober, he grew ever more uncomfortable and ill at ease. He imagined Beatie's tight lipped disappointment at the overcooked dinner and wished he had kept the flowers. He tried to picture his little golden-haired Sylvia Margaret as a fourteen-year-old and failed. His feet slowed, his whistle faltered as he finished the climb up West Hill and turned into Marcett Road looking for number 16.

He studied the quiet orderly street with the picture windows in the door frames. He marvelled at how this road, situated so close to the railway line leading to Biggin Hill, had escaped a bombing. He shuddered as the old memory of the whoosh and screaming roar of a direct hit swept through his mind leaving him unsteady with more than too much beer.

The suitcase waited on the front step as Cyril hesitated. This war had torn him into two men. There was plain old Cyril: husband Cyril and Cyril the father. That Cyril found this street familiar, warm, welcoming. The other one, Corporal Cyril, the Merry Whistler, was reluctant to pick up the brass knocker which would swing open a door to a world that no longer made any sense.

"Get on with it man!" he muttered, squared his shoulders, rapped hard and began to whistle, "The White Cliffs of Dover."

Sylvia Margaret was getting ready for bed when the knocker finally dropped followed by an echo of a half remembered past.

"It's Dad! It's his whistle! she said, flinging down the hairbrush.

"Wait." Auntie Betty laid a restraining hand on her elbow, "Let them say hello first and put on your dressing gown."

The raised voices, one deep the other sharp, drifted up through the ceiling. Sylvia Margaret and Betty exchanged a look. The conversation rumbled bad temperedly on before trailing off into an eerie silence.

"Oh dear," said Betty after a moment. "Let's get into bed. I'll put the radio on for a bit."

"But I want to see Dad." Sylvia Margaret continued to pull on her dressing gown, "and I want to have my celebration trifle like we planned."

"You'll just have to wait until the morning. It's too late for trifle."

"But Mum said. I really want to …"

"You aren't a little girl anymore." Betty was sharp. "You will just have to wait like the rest of us."

Sylvia got into bed without a word. For a while she faced the wall feigning sleep until her Aunt switched off the radio and turned down the lamp. She wanted to nestle into her Aunt's sturdy comforting frame and sleep as spoons, like they always did, but a residue resentment held her back.

"This is all Dad's fault," were her final thoughts before falling into a troubled sleep. "Mum is the one that snaps, not Auntie Betty. He's come home late and I'm the one in trouble. I wish he would go back to where he's come from."

Dad was still in bed when Sylvia left for school. All day she hoped he might be waiting at the gates. She imagined him handsome and in uniform like the picture on the mantlepiece. They would walk home together, arm in arm. He would whistle a marching tune and they would eat the trifle in double quick time. Instead, she went home as usual, with Gracie and Flo, inventing such fantastical stories about the homecoming and celebration trifle until she almost believed them herself.

Sylvia Margaret took off her blazer and hung her satchel on the peg, she kicked off her shoes and slid into the slippers Mum insisted on. At the farm in Norfolk, you could just go barefoot or not worry about a bit of mud, but everything was different here. And now it would be even more different.

All the voices were coming from the kitchen. Sylvia Margaret stood in the doorway. Dad was leaning over the table and demonstrating how something worked. Mum and Auntie Betty crowded round him, smiling and excited. At last, she was noticed. Dad gave a wide grin and said:

"Sylvie!" he gestured to the square box, "Come and see what I've bought for us."

It was a gramophone. The latest RCA Victor model she and Gracie had admired in the Co-op window last Saturday. Next to it was a neat pile of large flat discs in paper covers. The one on top was *You Do* by Vic Damone.

"Oh," Sylvia Margaret breathed, "can you play that one?"

"If you come and kiss your old Dad first."

Sylvia Margaret took one hesitant step into the room then stopped. She appraised this stranger, smart in a grey suit and red tie. He was not as tall as she remembered. His dark hair was very short and had streaks of grey. She glanced at Mum who nodded, a hand on his shoulder. Auntie Betty pointed the spoon she held at the bowl of trifle.

Dad began to whistle *Teddy's Bears Picnic*. Sylvia Margaret ran across and threw her arms round his neck. She inhaled the familiar scent of Brylcreem and Old Holborn and forgot all about the ruined homecoming party and the empty school gates. Dad was home now and so was she.

Handsome is as handsome does:
1948
Sylvia Margaret

The clock tower said five past three. It was never wrong. Or so her Mum always said. If it was right then Gracie and Flo were going to make her late for the Tea Dance. Sylvia Margaret swung her shoe bag by its string and squinted down the road looking for the Number 696. It had been hard enough getting Dad to agree. He said she was too young and the dress too bright and too short for a girl of fifteen.

It was chilly. She leant against the red brick wall, deciding to leave her cardigan off. The dress had elbow length sleeves with smart cuffs and ivory buttons. It was lovely. If Dad had his way she would be wearing khaki and not this gorgeous primrose yellow. He did nothing but bark out orders to the lot of them. She had overhead Auntie Betty whisper that they might as well be in the army.

"He needs his eyes tested!"

Sylvia Margaret flushed and looked up. "Who does?" she managed.

"Whoever has kept you waiting," said a handsome man with a single white stripe on his army sleeve. His dark blue appreciative eyes looked directly into hers. "Now I would always be on time, or early."

Sylvia felt herself redden again and turned away, making a big show of watching the bus that was just rounding the corner of High Street.

"Where are you going to my pretty maid?"

She waved frantically at her friends who were off the bus and waiting at the kerb to cross. "To the Tea Dance at the Town Hall." She mumbled without turning round.

"That's good. We're going there too, aren't we boys?" he said and stepped up close, his hand briefly grazing her arm. "Nice dress. I hope you're a good dancer because I am."

Sylvia moved away but not before she had inhaled the pleasing scent of his aftershave and had taken in the broad shoulders straining at his jacket.

"I thought we were going to the Swan in Dartford." One of his mates protested weakly.

"Later Private Saunders." The handsome face darkened then cleared. "Say hello to these lovely ladies. "That's handy, three of us and three of you. Let's call it fate."

Dancing with Kenny was like flying. Sylvia Margaret had never felt so fleet of foot or so brave. He taught her the new Swing Jive, expertly lifting, swinging, sliding her this way and that, only ever a hands breadth away. He could Jitterbug, Rumba and Quick Step as well as anyone she had ever met at the Sybil Marks Dance class. He was surprisingly smooth and quick across the floor for a man of his height and build. Sylvia watched the lumbering efforts of Eric and the other boy Charlie from the corner of her eye. They were more like those slow, solid old cart horses from the farm in Norfolk. He could sing too: *I don't want to set the world on Fire* had never sounded so silky and sultry, not even by the Ink Spots, as it did when he murmured, word perfect, into her ear. Oblivious to the desperate looks from her friends Sylvia Margaret let herself be floated around the dance floor until the final notes had faded and the Raffle was called.

On the walk to the bus stop they trailed behind the others. Kenneth tucked her hand under his arm as if she were a grown up and had her laughing until her sides ached. He joked about army life in a way Dad never did. He offered her a ride on his motorbike down to Broadstairs. He said he would take her to meet his big crazy family. Sylvia Margaret gaped with envy at the idea of so many brothers and sisters. She confessed that she hated being an only child; the only one to be worried about; the only one Dad could boss around as if still the little girl he had left behind.

When the bus came he swept her up into his arms and gave her the kind of kiss she had never imagined. The kind that had her friends desperately pushing away their suitors and stumbling up to the top deck horrified and embarrassed. Sylvia Margaret did not care. Part of her was still on the dance floor, her lips tingling and her heart thumping with the beginnings of something she thought might be called love.

She waved from the back seat until the corner hid Kenny from view. She turned, triumphant to her peeved companions.

"Isn't he just wonderful?" Sylvia bounced up and down. "Such a brilliant dancer. He can sing better than anyone in the hit parade too. Isn't he just the most handsome man you have ever seen?"

Gracie was silent and squinted through the grimy window out at the passing shops.

"He's just a show-off and a spiv." Flo was dismissive. "Handsome is as handsome does."

"What does that even mean?" Hot angry tears stung the back of Sylvia's eyelids. "You're just a sorry green- eyed, jealous bitch. That's what you are!"

She sprang from her seat and marched off. "I'm going to sit downstairs and think about *my* handsome man. That's what I'm going to do."

"And that's just what you'll be if you keep on with him." Flo called after her retreating back, "Sorry!"

The Big Freeze:
1963
Kaz

Kaz came in through the back door with her arms full of washing. Dad's trouser legs stuck out stiffly, frozen solid. Everything on the line was the same, the pegs cracking, sticking stubbornly to the clothes, reluctant to release their captives. Her hands were chapped red raw, her nose and ears stung with cold. Outside the early afternoon sky was a threatening slate grey, already smoke laden from chimneys lit early. It was almost as cold inside. The heater in the kitchen corner was belching out the sickly smell of pink paraffin but making little difference to the temperature.

Mum was sitting at the table with Auntie Doris, Cindy and Boxer the dog. They all had their coats on, even Boxer had one strapped beneath his substantial belly. He looked up at Kaz with his sad liquid brown eyes and dribbled a greeting.

"I'm going out with Doris," said Mum, "Look after Cindy."

It was then Kaz noticed that Auntie Doris, who was Mum's friend, not a real auntie, was drying her eyes with a cotton handkerchief with the letter D embroidered in the corner. Grandma Beatie had some with a B and Grandpa Cyril with a C. Kaz wished she had one with a K. She resisted wiping her nose on her sleeve, sniffing loudly instead.

Kaz liked to look at Auntie Doris. She admired her golden hair, almost always pinned up in what Mum said was a French Pleat. She had been a Tiller Girl before she married Uncle Bob and had danced for the Queen at The London Palladium. Today she had on a pair of knitted stockings and long boots with a heel and black gloves to match. She was a "glamour puss" Dad said and Kaz had agreed, adding stoutly that Mum was a "glamour puss too."

"Why are you crying Auntie Doris?" she said, her heart dropping a little as she saw a tear slip from beneath the thick fringe of dark lashes. Without thinking she dropped the slowly thawing clothes onto the floor and rushed to her side.

"It's 'cos Boxer's got to go," said Cindy. "'cos Boxer keeps eating the letters and my shoes, so he's got to go. My Dad said so."

"Go where?" Kaz lay a protective hand on the old dog's silken head.

"To the vet place, that's where," continued Cindy, "he's old and eats things so he's got to go."

Kaz no longer liked Cindy. Snivelling little pest. Let *her* go to the vet instead.

"What will happen to him?" she said.

"They will find him a nice home with a garden." Said Auntie Doris with a small insincere smile.

Kaz saw her eyes slide away. It was like when Dad said he was going to take Crackers to the vet if she had anymore kittens. There were two more hidden in the coal hole, wrapped in Grandma's old fur coat.

Auntie Doris tapped the Christmas presents with a long painted nail. "Why don't you put these under the tree." She said and stood up, smoothing down her skirt and tying a dark silk scarf around her shining hair.

"Alright." Said Kaz. "Come on Cindy."

As they reached the door Kaz said, "cats don't eat letters and shoes. You can have one of our kittens if you like."

"We'll see," Doris said. "That might be alright."

"One is brilliant white with blue eyes and the other is ginger with eyes the colour of…" Kaz paused searching for the correct word, "like…like yours…red and gold…like copper rings with flecks."

The two women laughed. "You're a real poet Kaz!" said Auntie Doris and rewarded her with a bright, tremulous smile. "We'll see." She said again.

Dad was in the front room with Uncle Bob. The fire was burning nicely, stacked high with coal and a big log on top. The two men sat either side of a low table, only inches away from the heat, their heads bent over the draughts board, bottles of brown ale, cigarettes and matches at their elbows.

"Come on Bob. Just put your namesake down. Best of three." Said Kenneth slapping down two sixpences, adding slyly, "or are you afraid of putting your money where your name is?"

For a few minutes Kaz and Cindy sat whispering beneath the tree, pushing around the presents, pressing them, feeling for clues until Dad said.

"Clear off you two. Go into the other room and make paper chains with the others."

"It's cold in there," protested Kaz.

"Clear off I said." Dad looked up, his fingers holding a piece to make a king. His face held that warning look. "Put your coat on. You don't see Cindy walking about in a skinny jumper do you?"

"Alright." Said Kaz. "Come on Cindy." Kaz paused at the door. "Uncle Bob?"

"What now?" said Dad.

"Can I give Auntie Doris one of our kittens? They don't eat letters or shoes."

Uncle Bob grinned, digging in a pocket for his shilling, "I don't mind."

"Now get out of here!" said Dad, "Or I'll chuck out that Crackers and her wretched kittens from the coal house."

By the time Mum and Auntie Doris got back a blizzard had begun. They shook off a thick layer of snow from their coats and scarves and ran to the heater to warm their hands. A few flakes were left on Auntie Doris's hair. She was tall, slim, glittering. Auntie Doris was lovely. Even lovelier than Mum.

"You can have a kitten." Kaz said gruffly, feeling a sudden shyness. "Uncle Bob said you can. I'll bring it round on Boxing Day. It will be big enough by then."

Boxing Day:

Everyone else was in the living room with the fire apart from Dad. He was in the kitchen lagging the pipes under the sink and swearing. They had frozen again. Outside the snow was already ankle deep. Kaz went through the front door, down the gully to the coal hole. She scrapped aside the snow, burning her woollen gloves, ice-scorching her fingertips. Crackers hissed and flung out an angry paw but Kaz evaded her reaching in for the ginger kitten. She wrapped him in an old school jumper, ran back and crept up the stairs. She slammed her door shut, flinging off her sodden pyjama bottoms and leapt into bed to read her new book, The Snow Queen, the tawny bundle in her lap. She hoped Auntie Doris still had some milk left. They had run out. Dad was swearing about that too and because all the sport had been cancelled, even the Dogs.

Every time she rubbed the steam from a window and looked out nothing had changed. The sky was a strange leaden grey with a long layer of black cloud. The snow fell straight down, like huge silent white stones. Finally she dressed, putting on an extra jumper and the red balaclava Grandma Beatie had knitted. She took Dad's work scarf from the bannister, covered Ginger with it then pushed him inside her donkey jacket. She could only find her sisters' Wellingtons but squeezed into them anyway then limped into the kitchen.

"I'm taking Ginger to Auntie Doris." She stated feigning confidence. It was dark and bitter and the snow too big and deep to be fun.

Mum was carving cold turkey and ham slices. Dad was sitting with his feet on top of the heater, peeling an orange.

"Don't be silly," said Mum, "You can't go out there. Wait til tomorrow."

"Ginger is a Christmas present so it's got to be today." Kaz insisted, adding with a quick look at Dad, "and they might have some milk I can bring back."

"Let her go." said Dad, "She's big enough and ugly enough."

"I really don't think…" began Mum but Kaz had already turned for the door.

"And don't forget that bloody milk!" Dad called after her.

At first, whilst she had the brick garden walls to hold onto she made good progress. The streetlights glimmered dimly above, serving as landmarks. The problems began when she tried to cross where she thought the road should be. She tripped on the hidden curb and sank knee deep. Away from the shelter of buildings the wind whipped at her, sending flurries of sharp snow splinters that stuck to her eyelashes and coated her eye lids. It was hard to keep upright, wipe the icicles away and hang onto the struggling kitten at the same time. Auntie Heather and Uncle Tom, two more of Mum's friends, were crossing the other way, their heads behind a straining umbrella.

"Is that you Kaz? Come back with us. We'll walk you home." Said Uncle Tom, taking her arm as her feet slithered and slipped from under her.

"No, thanks." She said, "Its Boxing Day and I've got a present for Auntie Doris."

"Take it tomorrow," suggested Heather, "What can't wait until tomorrow?"

Kaz shook her head. "It's Ginger and he needs some milk and we don't have any."

"Come on now…"

"Don't worry about me." Kaz waved them away and dragged herself forward, clinging onto the kitten for all she was worth. Dad said I'm big and ugly enough."

The wind stung and the snow spat. The darkened houses were grey shapes, their doors increasingly covered in thick banks of snow. Kaz laboured on. The walk was hard and long and lonely but somehow the solitary snow-filled night was beautiful. Each flake that settled on her arms were brief perfect ice flowers. Kaz felt a growing relief as, in between the gale driven gusts, the outline of Auntie Doris's block of flats became visible. On the outside all her extremities were frozen: her feet, her hands, her nose protruding from the knitted head covering, her stuck together lips, her ice-splintered weeping eyes.

On the inside a warmth was spreading, beginning where she supposed her heart might be. She was nearly there. When the door opened she would offer up Ginger, the copper eyed kitten, to Auntie Doris, who was as regal and royal and splendid as any Snow Queen.

The Rising Sun:
1965
Kaz

Kaz hated this skirt. She hated all skirts. This one though, was the worst, but Dennis had said:

"If you wear that skirt, the jean skirt with buttons down the front and your heel shoes I'll take you to Ramsgate on the train."

Kaz had looked at him hard. Why should he tell her what to wear just because he was her boyfriend but...?

"Ok but only cos I want to go to Ramsgate not because you said and," she had a sudden come back," you've got to wear that jumper with Elvis on and put Brylcreem in your hair."

They stood either side of the kitchen table and locked eyes. Finally, Dennis had nodded:

"Alright, but not cos *you* said either."

Kaz was almost regretting it. One of the buttons on the skirt was hanging, the hem had slipped at the back. Mum was never going to mend them now, probably not ever. Wearing it meant stockings and a suspender belt. She would need a sixpence for that fastening. Still American tan was a good look: an American look. If only she could wear her bobby socks and baseball boots not those cruel Sunday shoes. It was at least a mile from the station to the beach. Her feet would get blisters. When she had said that to Dennis he had just shrugged:

"You can take them off and walk barefoot," and as she had hesitated, he added, "I'll buy you six sticks of rock if you do."

Why was Dennis always going on at her about dressing like a girl? When had he started? It was when she had let him kiss her that time at the cinema and hold her hand all the way up Temple Hill for everyone to see. It had been a stupid old film too: *Seven Brides for Seven Brothers*. Kaz cringed at both memories, stepped away from the mirror and tuned to Radio Caroline.

From the window she could see the sky was grey June not flaming June like Grandpa Cyril always called it. "I hate these flaming clothes", she thought and at that moment, almost hated Dennis.

Dennis:

Dennis was in his bedroom getting ready. The faint sounds of *The House of the Rising Sun* drifted through from Kaz's room next door. He switched on his transistor liking the idea of them listening at the same time. The song reminded him of that pub on Ramsgate beachfront. Now he was eighteen he could take Kaz to *The Rising Sun*. If they sat in the corner, they would get away with it easy. If only she would grow her hair a bit more. Girls shouldn't have Beatle cuts.

On the ghost train he could put his arm round her. She would pretend to be afraid just because she was trying to be a girl for the afternoon. Kaz was not afraid of much and that was why he liked her. The other girls were silly and giggled at nothing, but she could talk to him about books and politics. He frowned. If only she would stop playing football on the green with Johnny Wilson and Fatty Hart. If only she would act like a real girlfriend all the time.

Dennis scraped up an extra-large handful of Brylcreem and rubbed it through his hair, took his comb from his back pocket and spent ten minutes getting the quiff just right. The Animals were onto "I gotta get outta this place." He looked at his birthday watch and rapped on the wall, waited then rapped again. At the return signal he picked up his jumper and leapt the stairs two at a time, patting his pocket making sure he had the train tickets and change for the rock he had promised.

The day was overcast and chilly. He had hoped for sunshine. He would give her his jumper; she would fake a scream on the Roller Coaster and clutch at his arm. He would order a Pale Ale and a Babycham at the bar when Dennis and Katrina; boyfriend and girlfriend; walked hand in hand into *The Rising Sun*.

The Midday Sun:
1966
Cricket

They were already choosing teams when Kaz arrived. She had run up most of Temple Hill to get there on time. It was her half day. Mr Berkley had let her go at quarter to twelve. She flourished her prized real cricket ball. It was probably the only way they would let her play, that and their uneven numbers. When had they begun not to want her, their best player? Since she had left school and had to wear dresses and skirts every day to the office? Or was it now she was Dennis's girlfriend? When exactly had they stopped thinking of her as just Kaz?

Reggie Spinks smirked as she stood in line waiting to be picked. He snatched the ball from her hand exhaling his dirty smelly breath into her face: "Are you sure you should play Kat.trin.a? Won't your bra strap slip?" Heat from the insult swept through her, melting into the scalding midday sun now definitely scorching the back of her neck. She never wore a bra, did not need to yet, hoped she never, ever would. They were for girly girls like Angie. Kaz had a fleeting memory of those soft breasts in her hands and the kisses under that dank dark bridge. This was quickly replaced by a picture of big boys with catapults; a mad dash through a slippery pond; a hair-raising hop skip and jump across the Puffing Billy line as the monster Goods Train hurtled towards them.

Kaz was given final bat and made to field at the far corners of the green. She knew it was unfair but her overwhelming desire to play stifled the protests that clamoured inside. It was a hot, hot, June day. A flaming one, like Grandpa Cyril always called it. Kaz wished she had a hat or even a dirty handkerchief tied at its four corners like Dad. The sun beat upon her neck, moisture began to form on her brow. Damp patches were already spreading under the arms of the too thick blouse.

She baked in the midday sun, impatiently watching the slow score creeping upwards, chasing every occasional ball that came her way. Reggie whacked wildly at a spinner sending it sky high. Kaz squinted into the cloudless blue, followed its spiralling progress downward and effortlessly caught it one handed.

"Howzat!" she yelled sprinting to pick up the bat he had flung aside. She marched to the crease, looking across at Johnny with expectant narrowed eyes. She was going to show them. Knock it for six and then some! Reg was down at the bowling end taking the ball from Johnny. Kaz smiled thinly. If he was going to bowl it was more like a half century before the sun went down. She dug the wood into the crease and checked her stance. She was ready. A few others joined Reg and Johnny. Finally, the small circle broke apart. Reg held the ball up and said with his best sneer:

"Green team declares, and we accept a tie!" For a half minute Kaz faltered in front of the wicket anticipating a protest from her team or at least from Johnny who was keeping his head down, his eyes on his shoes.

"You can't just do that." She said stamping towards them, the bat dangling from her hand.

"I can. I'm Captain and I can." Reggie's eyes glittered triumph. "It's too hot Kat..trin..a. It's too mad to play any longer." With a fierce sweep of his arm, he threw her ball; her special real cricket ball; deep into the tangled undergrowth. "Here catch that!" he said.

This time, Kaz could not choose to ignore their new otherness. The way their familiar faces grew hard and obstinate whenever she tried to claim her customary place in their games. She was no longer Kaz but Kat..trin..a; the female interloper: the alien insinuating herself into their all-male club. She dropped the bat and took a few steps away. There were muted sniggers and an outright jeer from Reg. Without conscious thought, only aware of the heat and the simmering injustice of the afternoon, she turned and delivered a sudden swift punch which caught him full on the mouth. There was a collective groan of disapproval, a stray laugh from Johnny, as Reggie fell backwards and rolled around in the dust, swearing, sobbing, a hand to his bleeding mouth.

"Here catch that," said Kaz and threw a parting kick at the bat before turning away. "Keep your stinking cricket Captain Stinking Useless."

She kept to a steady walk up the crescent into her road although her legs felt the urge to run. She thought about coming back later to find Uncle Bunny's ball and refused to let the tears get past her lashes. She sucked at her smarting knuckles and comforted herself with a replay of that right hook. She had hit stinky Spinksy for six alright.

The house was quiet and the living room dark, curtains flapped in the breeze from the open windows. The black and white images from the television flickered across her father's prone and sleeping form. There was cricket on. It was England and the West Indies. Twenty-two men in white trousers and the Umpire swathed in white jumpers sweltering in the sunshine. Kaz thought about their cricket pitch at school and no longer wondered why only the boys from across the road could play. If it *was* just a man's game why was she so good at it?

Dad stirred, pushed the newspaper from his face and said, "Who's winning?"

"West Indies." Kaz said and sat down beside him. She felt the back of her neck. It was burning. "My neck's got scalded playing cricket Dad."

"Go and run the dish cloth under the cold tap," Kenneth said, "put it on your neck. You'd better drink some squash and bring me that bottle of brown from the cold larder."

They sat for a while, watching the cricket together. Every now and then Kenneth reminded her to wet the flannel and drink her squash. He was in a rare good mood. He had a tenner on the Windies, they were miles ahead with only an Over to go.

"Reggie Spinks shut down our cricket before I got to bat." Kaz said, "He said it was too hot and declared a tie."

"Only mad dogs and English men play out in the midday sun." Dad said, pointing at the telly, "unless there's money on it."

"I caught him out, so he got his revenge."

Kenneth lowered the bottle and glanced at Kaz whose grazed knuckles were gripping the glass. "So, what did you do about that then?"

"I smacked him in the mouth Dad." Kaz said in a rush. "Do you think Mr Spinks will come round?"

Kenneth laughed. "I'd like to see that. The skinny runt. Still, you should give up playing games with those boys now you're at work. No one likes a girl who can beat them."

Kaz thought about that as she put on the kettle and opened the cans for tea. She thought again of those boys last winter in the park. She remembered Dennis's mood when she beat him at the bowling alley last Saturday. Boys were such spoilt babies.

Later as they all sat in the kitchen with their beans on toast, the door wide open, the heat still stifling, Kaz's neck still raging, Dennis jumped the fence and stood, diffident and shy, on the step.

"Coming out Katrina?" he said flushing at the smothered giggles from the three smaller girls.

Kaz put down her fork and looked up behind hooded lids. Boys were all such babies. They were all bossy and all bad losers. Even her Dad got mad if he lost a bet or his tea was late.

"No," she shrugged, "No. I'm tired and hot with all that midday sun."

"Come on in Dennis." Mum said, "Have you had your tea?"

"No!" Kaz said sharply. The table fell silent. Kenneth lowered his football coupon. Her mother began to open her mouth but Kaz jumped in quick.

"No thanks. Not tonight...not any night actually..." Kaz felt mean but also a small kernel of grim satisfaction grew as Dennis coloured to the roots of his hair and water began to fill his soft brown eyes. "I don't want a boyfriend anymore, so you'd better go and find someone who does."

Dennis lingered a second before turning away.

"I'll come back tomorrow," he mumbled thickly, "When you've got over your midday sun."

"Don't bother," Kaz yelled after him ducking a back hander from Dad as she scraped her chair on the new lino. "I don't want to be a girlfriend and it's not because of the midday sun either."

Sunset at Porthcawl:
24th October 2020
Extract from the diary of an Outlander

A trip to Porthcawl had not been my intention. I was heading for Barry Island. The motorway was strangely empty for a late Saturday. I forgot to follow the signs and took a wrong left turn. I considered the geography. It *was* on the border between Bridgend and Rhondda Cynon Taff. Also it was one of those serendipitous "hung for a sheep as a lamb" moments: too far to turn back, too near to resist.

The Irish Sea is still the Irish Sea whether in Whitmore Bay or Trecco Bay, just a bit further round the headland. So, I drove the few extra miles through the town's twists and turns, anticipating deep breaths of salt sea spray, wafts of golden chip butties and made plans involving a fresh supply of sweet sticky rock and the sipping of lukewarm tea. All these delights could be readily purchased at any one of the numerous beachside kiosks. They were outside and would be open for Takeaways. Despite the drizzle, the place would be peopled with masked, socially distanced locals, enjoying the first day of half term. The Welsh are philosophical about weather. They embrace it as much as curse it. Such was my optimism.

For once I was conveniently parked opposite the strip of sand close to the refreshments area. A sudden squall had transformed the mildly overcast autumnal sky into a dark and rain-heavy slate grey that merged into a moody green angry sea. Its white heads of foam topped enormous white horse waves rushing halfway up the beach before sulkily receding only to restart its relentless journey. Is this the "ebb and flow of human misery" described by Matthew Arnold in Dover Beach?

I wound down my rapidly steaming up window and listened to the satisfying roar of wind and crashing waves. The beach was pristine neither littered by plastic nor people save a few brave hearts in wet suits with surfboards. I imagined huddled groups in raincoats queuing good-naturedly at the far end under umbrellas; their offspring stamping wellingtons into puddles, sucking rock or chasing flyaway candy floss. I listened past the swell of wind and wave for the faint tinny music drifting through speakers from impromptu outdoor pub areas. I heard only the clanging knell of silence.

Nonplussed but undeterred I struggled into my raincoat and jammed on my beanie, shoving change into a pocket along with car keys. A quick walk down the ramp and then a stiff climb up into the cafe area revealed a desolate landscape. A Saturday afternoon ghost town. Every kiosk was shuttered and boarded, play areas sticky taped off: nothing open and no one to share my disappointment by that raised eyebrow or that shrug which has replaced the usual polite facial expressions of yore.

To say it was a sad sight would be an understatement. All these small businesses once again plunged into unemployment by an invisible virus – or by governments with only one idea. This October half term is always known by beach workers as the "last chance half term." The last chance to put a bit by before the great winter shutdown. The last chance to get ground rents paid and students to earn something extra. An old, battered sign swung in the wind, the metal shutters beneath rattling a mournful tune. I gave a very thin smile at the irony of the casino's name: *The Last Chance Saloon.*

I trod all the well-worn uneven pathways. I turned into every alley and every nook and every cranny hoping not just for one open cafe but for that elusive "just one open public toilet." There was nothing open and no one. Eventually I decided, as King Lear had once said, "Nothing comes from nothing." I went through some broken barbed wire into a piece of grubby undergrowth to relieve myself.

Three surfers flapped past me in rubber slip-on shoes; hair plastered to sleek heads, boards grasped in chapped hands. One laughed and waved, guessing, rightly, why I had sought out the waste ground. I pulled on my gloves and wound the scarf tighter round my neck. I could, at least, sample the salty air and gaze off into that invisible freedom called an English horizon. I *would* watch the sun, if any were to be had, go down.

I descended the concrete steps to the beach and followed the foot trails of the two other occupants. Matchstick imprints from wader birds and a pair of dog paws outnumbered any evidence of humanity. Someone, a woman I think, clothed head to toe in a long gabardine was talking into her mobile phone. She seemed to be taking video selfies using the mile-high waves as a backdrop. Why would that be better viewing than simply facing the sea and marvelling at the real thing?

Further along I saw something more interesting: the bent back of a man, bare headed in a checked fleece, beside a wheelbarrow of all things. I placed my feet into his boot prints and tracked my way to where he knelt. I lingered at a safe distance watching as he scooped up handfuls of seaweed into a big green sack. He was so engrossed in his task that it took a while before he noticed me.

"For the allotment," he said, pulling up his black mask with the yellow smile. "The old ones tell me it's the best thing for poor soil."

I nodded, remembering being told the very same thing by "an old one" in Skerries, Co Dublin, forty years earlier. "It is." I agreed and added as an afterthought, "Did you know Porthcawl means "harbour with sea kale?"

He shook his head, "I only know the beach is full of it and for once there's room for me to collect as much as I need."

"Good luck." I said, glad someone was getting something from this empty afternoon and went off to finish my walk before driving through Coney Island to take the quicker route home.

I was passing the Grand Pavilion intent on leaving my disappointments behind when I caught something in the corner of my eye: a huge white awning battered by the breeze and a wooden notice board tied to a metal bench:

"Pietro's Italian ice cream **WE ARE OPEN!**"

Well yes: I screeched to a halt, reversed into a space and leapt from the car. I bought an ice cream, a cup of not half bad tea, and asked for rock. I emptied my pockets of change and accepted a bar of pink and white nougat in lieu of rock. Grateful to buy anything, glad to give them the little I had. I ignored the wind slapping at my face; the wet immediately seeping into the seat of my jeans and perched on their bench looking out to sea cone in one hand, plastic cup in the other.

A weak globe of light suddenly emerged from a bank of black cloud. I waited until that fragile sun slowly sank down over the yardarm of a stray fishing boat anchored to a bobbing orange buoy. This too shall pass" or so says the Sufi wisdom story. A hint of hope from *Sunset in Porthcawl*.

Beyond the Veil:
23 December 2020
Extract from the diary of an Outlander

We stuff our masks into pockets and step a little further apart.
A little closer to the glass doors. She is seated upright in an
armchair on wheels, stiff and still as a statue. We fix our
smiles. We search the eyes for a spark, a glimmer of
recognition. They do not flicker nor blink. She is somewhere
beyond the veil gazing off into an unknown horizon. Already I
am feeling the frustration grow. I fear these artificial visits:
hate the window that takes us yet another step further away.
I question the apparent necessity of its inhumane cruelty. I
unfairly resent the intrusive presence of the Care Assistant.
"Give me the mask and the gown and the blue gloves" I think,
"she is mine, not yours."

"Hello!" we call. Over-loud, over-bright and then repeat in
French, "Bonjour!"

There is no response, of course. We exchange a desperate
look. Erica embarks on the French nursery rhymes that
worked last time. I falter along with my imperfect accent. We
only have three and they are soon finished. We trail off, the
Assistant shrugs embarrassed, as if it is her failure.

"She's having a quiet day," she says, "No English, no French.
No joy, I'm afraid."

A bright memory comes swift. She used to call me her "joie"
and charm the night away with the language of love: *Je t'aime
pour toujours; mon amor; ma cherie; mon ang.* I press my face
to the glass and search for the one sentence I remember, the

one she would leave on the table for me to find or dash off on a postcard or whisper into the telephone: *vous me manqeuz.*

I turn to Erica and question: "miss you?" She expands the phrase: "Tu me manques" then adds, "Tu nous manques" "we miss you." I am grateful. Without Erica 's French there would be one more barrier, probably one barrier too many.

I brandish the brown paper bag that contain my ridiculous Christmas gifts: a bottle of Dandelion and Burdock, a packet of Quavers, a tube of chocolate buttons, strawberries cut and soaked in sugar the way she likes, a card with a robin and a message inside that she can no longer read.

Another sudden memory arrives. One Christmas Eve she had presented me with a hundred newly minted pound coins in a red velvet bag with a finely plaited gold drawstring. When she had asked what I wanted I said, "A bag of gold would be good." Now as then, I laughed out loud.

She was a woman that always surprised. Always kept you guessing. Mr Alzheimer's as she used to call that wretched disease, had taken us both by surprise. I look hard through the glass fearing this might be the day of the total eclipse. I search for the woman I love. Her eyes are blank yet still a startling sapphire like those of the White Tiger I had admired in Singapore Zoo that first year she was truly lost. His eyes *were* distant but wild, huge paws forever pacing, pacing, pacing behind that transparent barricade: looking for that horizon lost in the blink of a bright blue eye.

We stall. Alzheimer's, COVID and windows are winning as they always do. I fumble through my pockets for our fallback position: iPhone and YouTube. Music has often lifted the veil.

But we had been inside then. Had sat next to her. Held her hand. Had been able to give and receive the gift of touch.

We indicate hopefully at the nearest window. It is opened an inch. I turn up the sound and we go through our repertoire: beginning with Kathleen Ferrier's *What is Life*.

"You like this one," shouts Erica valiantly, "We used to sing it in the office...remember?"

We exchange a look. "No," she says, crestfallen. "Of course, she doesn't."

"No, but you do." I say, "that counts. Let's try *Santa Baby*."

We try *Santa Baby*. We try *In the Bleak Mid-Winter* and finally, *Here comes the Sun*. We bravely sing along. The veil has always lifted before, those eyes eventually settling on one of us. Finally, her gaze slides from me to Erica and then back to me. We hold our breaths. My hands go instinctively to the window as if I can vaporise it and will words from her tired mind.

She begins to projectile vomit in the way a baby might. Her eyes stare into mine, no longer blank but puzzled then apologetic. I rattle the door handle and shout useless instructions. As she is hurried away there are a thousand memories of her comforting hand on my shoulder, her fingers caressing the back of my neck, her words "hush my sweet love," "chut mon doux amour." They drift beyond the veil, elbowing Mr Alzheimer aside, making light of COVID19, windows and all else.

I step away horrified but oddly relieved. So today is not to be the total eclipse of my heart...not quite...

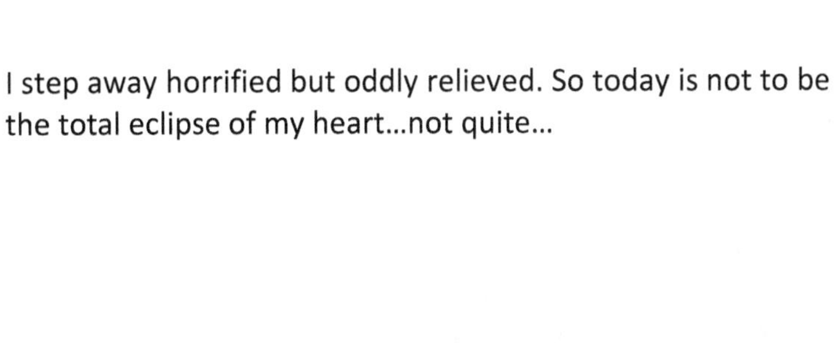

For as long as it Takes:
Jockey Jones
1988

Jockey had stealthily packed the suitcase for over a week. She had clock watched all day; her mind only half on the customers, impatient for the magic number five. Now, she hopped on her bicycle and headed for home with just a casual wave to the others. Her head was already busy with what else could be taken or discarded: what there was room for and what there was not. There was no way she could take her Boom Box but the tapes were possible: at least her precious Salt-N-Pepa; Boy George and The Pet Shop Boys. She pedalled hard uphill humming *Push it* then careened down the breath-taking slope, her feet off the pedals, singing an off-tune rendition of *Sussudio.* Yes there had to be room for one Phil Collins. Was it still played in all the clubs? Jockey skidded to a halt outside the back door with an image of her dancing self: red leather jacket open, tight white T and baggy blue jeans: the coloured strobe lights flashing circles on the dance floor, the music leaping off the walls, the eyes of all the girls on her. All the pretty girls looking like all the best sweets in all the best sweet shops. It was a constant image she had carried with her since the day she had made up her mind. A bright clear and definite image. An unshakeable image. A non-negotiable image.

She ran upstairs and began to fill the case some more. It was getting a bit too heavy for heaving up and down off the wardrobe. Jockey thought about where she could hide it. But then, out of nowhere, came the thought: Why wait? I've got the money for the ticket and a weeks' holiday from tomorrow so I won't be putting Dad out at the shop. Then another thought struck her: Why wait til tomorrow? There was a seven o'clock train going to Paddington, she would arrive by ten. It was Summer, the days were long, the light slow to fade. How hard could it be to find somewhere for the night?

Within ten minutes the packing was complete, her blue denim jacket on, cash deep into her back pocket. Jockey bumped the case down the stairs and into the kitchen. Mum was cooking tea, her back turned to the stove. Dad was sitting at the table, shirt sleeves rolled up, tie off, reading the paper. For a moment she faltered. It was all so ordinary, familiar, and safe. *They* were so ordinary, familiar, and safe. The bright, clear image returned with a vengeance.

"I'm off to London." She said and waited. Her face a mask of airy confidence.

"Oh?" said Mum, "Who with? You didn't say. You could've said."

 "I've been thinking about it for a bit." Jockey shrugged. I'm going by myself."

"By yourself?" Dad lowered the paper. "Alison love. What kind of holiday will that be? You don't know anyone in London."

"It's not a holiday." Jockey squared her shoulders. "I'm leaving home. Today."

"What!" said both parents together and then fell silent. "Oh, I see." Said Dad eventually, "Very funny. Another one of your little jokes."

Jockey shook her head and defiantly ignored the glint of tears beginning behind her mother's eyes.

"What's this all about?" said Dad pushing aside his paper and standing up.

"It's about me." Jockey picked up all her worldly goods. "There's a bus to the station in ten minutes."

Mum turned down the potatoes and left the stove. "How long for then?"

Jockey paused and thought carefully about that question. "For as long as it takes."

"How long it takes for what?" said Dad.

"For as long as it takes to find …" Jockey searched inside that bright clear image. "For as long as it takes to find *me.*"

Dad sighed, took his jacket from the back of the chair. "I'll give you a lift then." he said. "That's a bloody heavy suitcase you've got there."

At the station Mum said, "Come back soon."

Dad said, "You'll be back in a week."

"It will take longer than a week." Said Jockey clambering up the step and into the train. "Like I said it will take as long as it takes."

She slid the case under her seat and went back to the corridor. As the train began its slow shunt away she leaned out and waved until they were no more than stick-figures. Watching whilst they and her childhood quickly receded into the distant past.

*

This was the first time Jockey had ever taken a train further than the nearest town. And that town was no more than a slightly bigger version of their village. Its' biggest attractions a dilapidated Scala cinema, an indoor swimming pool and a Woolworths. For a while she stared out wide-eyed as each passing scene disappeared replaced with another and then another less familiar than the last. There was obviously a big wide world out there. Why *had* she taken so long to break her chains?

As the golden dusk began to fade the scenery turned ugly. Waste ground and graffiti strewn concrete soon lost their alure. Jockey fell into a restless doze until the train shuddered to an unexpected halt, jerking her awake. She reached for her bag. No one else made a move. They merely turned another page of a newspaper or carried on with their muted conversations. The young couple opposite unwrapped a sandwich and split open a packet of crisps on the dividing table. Jockey was hungry, her stomach rumbled so loudly she blushed and resolutely turned her eyes away from their picnic.

"There's a buffet car further up," the man said.

"Oh, alright. Thanks." Said Jockey, unsure what that might mean. Food, drink, obviously. She hesitated, remembering the bulging cardboard suitcase under her seat.

"Don't worry," he said, "every train gets stuck in Didcot Parkway." He gave a friendly toothy smile.

"No-one's going to run off with it. This place is a road leading to nowhere."

Paddington was definitely a road leading somewhere. Jockey, enthralled, slow-walked the endless platform, dragging her case a few inches above ground level. The intimidating glass dome towered above. She felt herself shrink. Ahead was the teeming concourse. So it was true then: Londoners lived life like a smoking gun. The station clock dwarfed all else, reminding her of the News at Ten picture of Big Ben. Its huge black arrow clicked to five past the hour. In the distance an arch with a gigantic red circle and blue letters stating Paddington Underground beckoned.

Jockey stood frozen midway between train and tube. The unseeing masses darted to the left and right. She was struck by an elbow, the sharp edge of a bag, a huge bouquet of flowers. She was too small. Too insignificant. Too unseen. Now was the time to turn round, forget her big ideas and catch the 125 Inter-City back to where she belonged. Maybe this *was* as long as it takes? Perhaps the girl from the village was the only *Me*?

"Can I help Miss?"

Jockey lifted her head. A tall spare black man in the familiar grey of British Rail said, "You want the tube or the train?" Their eyes met. His were a deep brown and kind.

It was on the tip of her tongue to say "train" but instead the words "tube please" came out in a strangled gasp.

"I'll carry your bag down the steps and show you where to buy your tickets." He said and lifted it as easily as if it held nothing but cotton wool.

Jockey obediently trotted behind him, trying to keep up, mutely nodding her thanks when he left her by the kiosk. She stared aghast at the unintelligible map full of different coloured lines snaking every which way. She flinched at the gusts of warm, slapping wind. Flinched once more at the piercing screaming roar that travelled upward from the steep downward escalator.

She wavered. Turned towards the kiosk, away and then back. Finally, she closed her eyes and pushed a splayed hand at the board. Through lowered lids she dimly made out the blue line of Piccadilly just shy of her little finger and the station Ealing Broadway beneath her thumb.

"Single or Return?" said the woman behind the glass.

"What?" said Jockey, non-plussed.

"You going to stay? Or going and coming back?"

It was on the tip of her tongue to say "Return" but instead the word "Single" blurted far louder than intended. The woman snatched up the crumpled fiver Jockey had pushed beneath the partition and shoved ticket and change back with a frown.

"Sorry…" Jockey began to frame an apology but trailed off as the Booking Clerk impatiently shook her head and yelled "Next!"

"Mind the Gap!"

Jockey flung the bag ahead of her and made the desperate leap just as the whistle blew and the doors slid shut. It was past ten thirty but the carriage was full. It *was* true. London never slept. She sat on the edge of her case, pressing her thighs firmly either side. She had never come off a horse but this was more like riding a bull in a rodeo! She swayed back and forth and gave up trying to see anything through the filthy windows. She concentrated on counting off the stations from the map above her head.

The streets of Ealing Broadway were breathtakingly busy. Jockey looked about her dazzled. People littered the pavements. Cars and late-night buses crawled bumper to bumper. They were all going somewhere. But where was she going? She was suddenly aware of the hammering heart inside her jacket and the quick beat of a pulse at her wrist. Dizzy with hunger, tiredness, and something akin to panic she studied both sides of the street. Where were all the B and B signs of her imagination? Or the convenient taxi with the nice driver who would know all the best places to stay?

"Can we help you Miss?"

Jockey felt a steadying hand on her elbow. A middle-aged couple had formed a protective shield against the non-stop rush of bodies going in and out of the station entrance.

"Are you lost?" the woman, who still held onto her arm said, "Or are you unwell?"

"Not lost exactly," Jockey said slowly, gathering her wits, calmed by their uncanny likeness to her own parents. "I just need to find somewhere to stay that's all," adding, not quite untruthfully, "I've arrived a few days earlier than planned."

"West Ealing is the place for B and B's. Will that do?" The man glanced at his wife, who nodded decisively.

"I'm George and this is my wife Doreen." He lifted her case. "We can walk you as far as the taxi rank. Blimey Riley!" he set it down again with a grunt. "Brought the kitchen sink with you?" he said taking a firmer grip before briskly leading her further along the road towards her new life.

*

Jockey came home for a week at Christmas. Mum put her head round the bedroom door. "You've only been here a week love. What about the New Year? Your Auntie May is coming over."

"Got to get back." Said Jockey, rubbing a bit more gel into her spikey blond cut before carefully wrapping her boom box into a carrier bag and pulling on her Parker. She shoved her money into a pocket. Sweets went into another. Train ticket, Underground pass, and keys to her shared flat into a third.

Dad was at the kitchen table with his crossword. "Not found *me* yet then?" he said licking the tip of his pencil.

"Not quite Dad." She said with a half laugh, thinking that joke was wearing thin. "Just taking as long as it takes."

Her brother looked up from his comic and said with a sly grin: "What's a three-letter word beginning with G that used to mean happy?"

Jockey mouthed a "Fuck off" and kissed Mum goodbye.

"You'll be back in a week!" Dad called after her.

This time she caught the bus to the station. The train stuck at Didcot Parkway. Jockey sighed and pushed herself further down the seat and covered her chilled ears with her hood. She still missed her big hair. Another forty minutes and she would be home.

The Brass Jug (Part One):
Elora Ilos - Age 19

The Receptionist barely glanced at Elora. She waved without a word, at the line of plastic chairs shoved hard against the damp whitewashed brick. Elora joined the queue of other applicants and threw herself down. What was it with Receptionists? Cow.

She examined her competition from lowered thickly mascaraed lids. They were clones: definitely. All in a blouse and pencil skirt just below the knee. All with a blond, brown, or black bob hair cut; faint eye shadow; faint lipstick. She smoothed down her jeans, kicked her scuffed pair of diesels out of sight wishing she had got round to getting her split ends and roots done. The girl next to her flinched. What did they have to be so stuck up about? There was nothing clever about being a chambermaid or whatever it was called these days. It all boiled down to being a skivvy and being left no more than a twenty pence tip in the ashtray after spending days cleaning their toilet.

The others seemed to be captivated by a series of "Llandrindnod in its Heyday" sepia toned photographs opposite. She squinted across but the lighting was so poor it was hard to tell if they held any real interest. Despite its name, it was an awful old-fashioned hotel, even for this equally old fashioned once famous spa town. The Grand, it definitely was not. She opened the brochure she had brought with her: "A four-star bygone experience." "The best mid Wales has to offer." Bygone alright. The best? Poor old mid-Wales then.

They waited an hour. Elora fixated on the lopsided old railway station clock and counted her life away in seconds, minutes, quarter hours. At last, a door opened. The seated queue leaned forward, expectant.

"Not you," said the Receptionist coolly. "They aren't ready for *you* yet."

One of them muttered an apology. The others gave small self-effacing smiles. Elora thought:

"Bugger this for a game of soldiers. I'm going for a fag."

She reached under the seat for her bag. One of its tassels had wound itself round a leg. She pulled, swore then finally dragged it free. She stood with a vague gesture at the flickering yellow Ladies sign halfway down the corridor. Once inside she pushed open the window as far as the grill would allow taking a cigarette from her last packet of Regals. She stared into the flyblown mirror over the sink, where a tap endlessly dripped, and expertly recoated her lips with Scarlet True Velvet before counting to five. She took a deep breath and counted another five just to be sure.

Yes. She was sure. She flicked the dog-end through the window, nodded to her reflection and slung her bag over a shoulder. Where was even one good vibe? All was dismal and hopeless right down to the dark unpolished mahogany furniture and the discoloured Welsh slate beneath her feet. There was a definite smell of disappointment emanating from staff and guests alike. No one in their right mind would want to spend the next six precious weeks of their life in this throwback to Miss Haversham's living room. They should ditch the four-star sign for a crest over the front door saying: "Abandon all hope ye who enter here." No one and nothing of any value deserved such a fate. There were always jobs at one of the chippies in Barry.

Elora kicked open the door and hurried up the remainder of the corridor in search of an exit. The grim-faced Concierge who had brought them to Reception must have known a shortcut. She did not recall trolling through this labyrinth of twists and turns. It reminded her a little of the Hampton Court Maize, only made of wood and stone. She had got lost there too but at least then she could push through a few privets to freedom.

Finally, she came to a drab velvet green curtain with a paper sign "Private" pinned to it. She did not bother to count five, just drew it aside and skipped through regardless.

"Oh," she gasped, dazzled by the low-slung glass chandelier that glimmered above. Apart from a scuffed leather armchair and a threadbare red and gold Persian rug in front of an unmade fireplace the room was empty, thick curtains pulled against the bay window and the side street beyond. Elora did not count five before she stepped onto the rug and crossed to the mantelpiece. She picked up a silver framed photograph and put it down quickly. It looked like the Queen and that Philip. "Sorry Ma'am." She said stepping back with a sham curtsey. The only other object was an ornate brass pitcher that glinted at her dully in the half light. It held a bunch of dusty plastic flowers. She leaned closer. "Poor thing." She upended the ugly bouquet onto the floor then lifted it high for a better look. "You deserve a good clean with Brasso" she said.

She held her breath and listened as feet clattered on the stone floor outside, paused then moved on. Still holding the jug, she scanned the room for a way out. No helpful door. She would never get those old window frames open without a sound. Carefully she pulled the curtain an inch. No one. She cocked an ear. Nothing.

As a rule, Elora was a law abiding, never take a thing that isn't mine, kind of girl. Nevertheless, her free hand went unbidden to the buttons on her trench coat, opened the top two and thrust the jug inside. She neglected to count five, ignored its cold and accusing presence as she pinioned it under her armpit. A fleeting thought of "Why?" was rapidly replaced with "Why the hell not?" With a thumping heart, a sweeping wave of elation making her lightheaded, she strolled round the very next corner, through an open fire door that led to the car park. And there, nestled inside the coat, the brass jug remained for the entire long and tedious journey on the bumpy old Edwards coach destined for Cardiff student land.

End of Part One

The Brass Jug (Part Two):
Elora Ilos – Age 29

Elora stepped back from the long dresser mirror, stared hard at her reflection: the black narrow jeans, the knee-high leather boots; the white sleeveless T with "The Missfits" inked inside an outline of a guitar; the brand-new heart shaped tattoo on her right upper arm and finally the swing and the shape of her shoulder length orange and blond cut. She turned away, counted to five then looked back. Something was still wrong. She examined every inch of her image before counting another five. This time a slow smile spread across her face. She bent at the waist grabbed each rip on each leg and pulled hard until the holes revealed complete kneecaps. That was better. That was rock chic enough for this Gig: very Suzi Quatro or better still, very, very Blondie.

An impatient horn sounded sharply just outside. Elora went to the window and signalled she was coming. Her purple Fender Stratocaster already tuned for the first number was inside its case. Her fingers curled around the grips ready to snap the locks safely shut but then relaxed. She sighed, shrugged, leant across and gripped the cone-like stem of the brass jug, spilling the dried wildflowers as she took it from the windowsill. Without counting to five, without asking "Why" she wrapped it in an old scarf and placed it next to the guitar and muttered "Why the hell not."

The journey was as long and as tedious as Elora remembered. The van, if anything, was less comfortable than the Edwards coach. No one was in the mood for talking much. Probably too hung over or stoned from the night before and the night before that. Elora desperately wanted a cigarette but hunted for nicorette gum instead. She dragged the packet from the inside pocket of her leather jacket and frowned at what looked like a folded page of newspaper stuck to it.

The cutting was folded neatly into four and was thin and yellowed with age. A dim, far off bell began to ring as she held it to the window for a better look. The headline in bold: ***Precious heirloom stolen from prestigious hotel*** clanged loud and long. How could she have forgotten? After all she had scrupulously cleaned the darn thing nearly every week for a decade. Anyway, she had *not* stolen it, merely borrowed it, liberated it from a life of neglect and now she was bringing it back.

Elora refolded the paper and returned it to her jacket. She leant her head against the window and closed her eyes, chewing vigorously, trying not to think about the real taste of nicotine. Instead for the first time in ten years she asked the question: "Why?" Nothing leapt out at her, just a jumble of seemingly unconnected fragments of memory: her mother's rare peel of laughter echoing in the night air of a car park. A roll of something large and bulky being hurried into the house and up the stairs. Holdalls and carrier bags unpacked in the middle of the night. Goods and money changing hands. The words "liberated" and "why the hell not?"

Briefly she drifted into sleep. Her dreaming mind chasing after the lost sound of her mother's laughter; the fragile joy of her childhood; a fallen figure in a narrow hallway. Then a faraway sound of a siren. Elora jerked into wakefulness, blinking as the ambulance, blue light flashing, weaved through the traffic as the van turned into the car park of The Grand.

Nothing much had changed. She sniffed the stale air and wondered at anyone choosing it as a wedding venue. The

Receptionist, somewhat older and stouter, graced them with a thin distant smile and led the way to a cramped and dingy room behind the stage of a faded ballroom. After ten minutes Elora left the others setting up the Amps with a vague gesture at the still flickering Ladies sign. No one remarked that she carried her guitar case. Elora never left her beloved "Strat" anywhere, with anyone.

The toilet was the same too. The same dirty window with the outside grill; the flyblown mirror in which she liberally coated her lips with Anastasia dusty orange gloss; the same drip, drip from a broken tap. She counted to five and then another five to be sure then gave the stiff wooden door a swift kick, turned into the corridor taking random right and left turns until she came to the paper sign "Private" still pinned eschew on the green velvet curtain.

All was as before: the glimmering chandelier, the worn Persian rug, the empty grate, the mantelpiece with the silver framed royal photograph. Elora did not stop to count five but stepped boldly across the carpet to examine a rather fine hand painted porcelain bowl full of faded lavender and chamomile pot pourri. "You poor thing." She upended the ugly remnants onto the floor lifting it high for a better look. "You deserve a good wash in fairy soapflakes." she said.

She held her breath and listened as feet clattered on the stone floor outside, paused then moved on. She lay her case on the carpet and clicked open the catch with her free hand pulling out the brass jug by its cone-like stem. "There you go," she said, "say hello to Queenie."

Apart from that rare slip, Elora was a law abiding never take a thing that isn't mine, kind of girl. Nevertheless, without a conscious thought or a counting to five her hand wrapped the porcelain bowl in the scarf and placed it where the brass jug had so recently nestled.

With a thumping heart, a sweeping wave of elation making her lightheaded, she strolled around the very next corner, through a fire door that led to the car park. She slid open the van door, took out her guitar and pushed the case beneath the back seat. Later as the flat tyred hire van bumped its long, torturous way back to Cardiff, Elora, her feet firmly atop the case, had the fleeting thought, "Why?" which was rapidly replaced with "Why the hell not?"

Once again she dozed, her head against the window. Her dreams chasing the lost sound of her mother's laughing echo in the night air of a car park.

The Fairy Godmother:
Georgina
March 2020

Georgina poured another cup of tea she did not want and ate the third chocolate biscuit she should not eat. If only she could get used to the silence that seemed to fill every corner in every room. Even with double glazing you would expect to hear something. Wouldn't you? She gave up on the tea and deliberately snapped the lid back on the biscuit tin, crossed to the French doors and put her face close to the glass. Everything was cloaked in grey: an almost total eclipse of light and life. No moon now, not even the North Star or the distant sodium glow of a streetlamp.

It was after three, one of those awful hours where she had read grief always lives, a dark night of the
soul moment all the bereaved must endure until the world begins to right itself. And it had begun to. Until this unseen virus and a disconcerting letter from Boris Johnson, of all people, had struck at the heart of what was left of her life. How was she supposed to stay in all day, every day, give up Aquarobics; the art class where she had made new friends. Struggle to learn to use WhatsApp. Live without her grandchildren's weekend hugs and kisses?

On her way back to bed she took a prudent stop off at the bathroom. Reflected in the mirror above the sink were the boxes stacked in the bath still waiting to be unpacked. For months she had barely glanced at them. On a whim she lifted the lid of the one nearest. Her heart gave an unaccustomed leap of pleasure. It was like a little bright light had suddenly switched itself back on. Inside was the first fairy grotto she had made with her very first class of five-year olds ever so many years ago. The paint had faded on the paper Mache figures. A few fairy wings were drooping but a bit of glue and acrylic paint would put that right. The backdrop of blue sky and impossible pink fluffy clouds had been done by Peter. He had always indulged her love of magic and belief in the little fairy folk. Sometimes she had thought he was a secret believer especially when he watched the gradually brightening faces of even the most withdrawn and sad child.

Georgina got back into bed and prepared herself for more wakeful hours: that inevitable counting off all her losses on both hands. Instead, she soon drifted into sleep and dreamed of dancing fairies, toy railways, elves and gingerbread men made from MDF. Her instant thought on waking was Peter's good-natured grumbles about his wrecked jigsaw blade and his wide smile once she had finished each project. Her second thought was to forget breakfast for now and go back to the bathroom, take a second look into that box for the long cardboard rainbow, folded into three at the bottom. The NHS certainly deserved a rainbow. It would fit nicely along the side wall in the front garden.

Breakfast was only remembered when it was time for lunch. The rainbow was faded, tattered and mouse nibbled. Georgina decided to salvage a few panels from the fence felled in a freak February wind and make a better more durable one. Another bright little light switched on. Why not turn the fairy grotto into a hospital ward with angel doctors and nurses? She added a dozen packets of extra-long Swan matches to her Tesco online shopping list. They would make the perfect base for miniature hospital beds.

A half-eaten sandwich and a cold cup of coffee languished on the kitchen counter as Georgina cut and snipped, glued and painted. Before she realised, it was past eight, dusk was quickly fading into night when the telephone finally broke the spell. It was Debbie.

"Hi Mum. Just thought I'd find out what you've been up to."

"Oh, this and that," Georgina said strangely reluctant to admit to starting a new garden project. It would be the first one since... since all those bright little lights had seemed to go out all at once.

She exchanged other news with her eldest daughter, her free hand busy trawling through scraps of material for bed covers and nurse uniforms. The back of her mind was still away with the fairies. Her eyes strayed to the wooden rainbow drying across the sink unit. Yes. All seven colours were correctly in place according to: *Richard of York Gave Battle in Vain.*

"So, we thought we might come down on Sunday afternoon and wave from the garden." said Debbie, "Although I don't know how Angharad will react to not being allowed indoors."

"That's alright love." Georgina quickly calculated the work left to do, including the setting up of solar lights. "I'll have something in the garden to distract them by then.

The weather was extraordinarily good for March. Georgina wondered if it was heaven, or at least fairy sent. Her afternoons flew by as she carefully put together her rainbow garden. In the beginning just a child or two, bored without their playground, stopped by with exhausted parents. As word spread Georgina would stand a safe two metres as small groups came to take a tour. Older boys and girls on scooters and bikes slowed as they went past shouting: "Cool!" and "Ace!" Nothing was ever stolen or broken.

By the end of the first lockdown the rainbow garden, to her surprise, had become the focal point for the Thursday Clap the NHS. Those two minutes often continued well into the warm evenings as neighbours who had lived side by side for years took the time to get acquainted. With every week that passed Georgina would linger on her front step chatting to whoever stopped by, finally closing the door feeling as if another bright little light had found its way home.

At the beginning of May when a certain kind of half-freedom beckoned Georgina waved her magic paint brush and created a sea, sand, and sun garden. A strip of blue was peopled with pixie swimmers and fairy sail boats. The sand sported a clockwork Merry-go-Round and swings. The backdrop was a sun with a huge smile on its yellow painted face.

When the October firebreak was announced Georgina gave the original fairy grotto another makeover. An impressive Fairy King and Queen were installed on thrones under a canopy of luminous gold stars. Little girls in fairy dresses daily crouched on the grass chatting to the royal occupants. As the nights drew in, she decked trees and shrubs with hopeful red, blue, green, and silver fairy lights. The rainbow reappeared, a lantern at each end.

November was more than midway through before she noticed. There seemed to be nothing but rain and more bad news whenever she turned on the television. Georgina put on her waterproofs deciding Christmas should come early to Tylwtyh teg Dell. She spent hours online and more money than she could afford adding to her already large collection of

Christmas ornaments. As she unpacked each remaining box another bright little memory would pop out. She worked steadily on, often with an umbrella overhead, oblivious to all the unusual activity taking place from neighbouring gardens.

Eventually the glass swan had been placed on the icy lake, the smallest reindeers rearranged one more time and her oldest friend, the polar bear, was given a new battery-lit necklace. She picked up her mallet and hammered home the signpost pointing the way to The North Pole, Lapland and Reindeer Crossing.

"When is your big Switch On?" A grinning man in a red jumper and a Santa hat slowed his car and called from the window.

Georgina had not thought about an official Switch On. She still had the complicated snowflake projector to set up but she smiled back at the man and his identically dressed little boy in the back seat and said:

"Is tomorrow at 6pm too soon?"

"Great idea." he said "There's a clear frosty sky predicted. Tomorrow will be a perfect night for it."

Georgina opened her door at five to six and looked up into the cloudless night sky. A cold enigmatic half circle of moon smiled down at her. It *was* a perfect night. But where had all these extra cars come from? And who were all these unfamiliar faces collecting in front of her **Santa Stop Here** sign? She did a double-take and looked about her with fresh eyes. Furniture was being hefted through side gates and onto pavements. Tables were filling up with wine bottles, flasks, glasses, mugs, bowls of sweets, packets of crisps. Children were running around lighting up the dark with spitting sparklers, their laughter echoing up and down the Dell. Her watch alarm buzzed. Georgina switched on and waited to see what would happen next.

A bell rang out. An impossibly young Santa began a shouted countdown followed by: "Alexa, play Jingle Bells!" A perfectly synchronised kaleidoscope of colour lit up every household in turn, cascading down the Dell as far as the eye could see. She gasped. The beautiful and the frankly garish blended together in a harmony of light and colour. Crackling wood burners offered up their yuletide orange flame; stars twinkled from windows; golden flashing bells from walls. Every tree and shrub became instant magical shadowy shapes of red, green and all the colours in between.

An impromptu procession had begun to follow all the bright little lights up and down both sides of the road and into the Crescent. The urge to join in was irresistible...If only Peter was here.

"Would you care to stroll round with me?" said a very elderly gentleman tipping his cap, gripping his wheeler with his other gloved hand. "I'm Sidney from number five." He offered an elbow. "I want to make sure not one house is overlooked or remains unadmired."

"I was just thinking the same," said Georgina. They gently bumped elbows and stepped into the slow-moving crocodile. "Do our roads usually go to town like this?" she said.

Sidney shook his head and stopped to point out the blow-up Santa halfway up a chimney. "Not in the five years I've been here. It's only ever been the odd wreath or a string of tree lights."

"Who *are* all these other people?" Georgina gestured to her right and left. "There must be the entire estate here."

"*Face Book*" said Sidney. "The *Community Face Book* page. Aren't you on it?"

Georgina shook her head. "I've been too busy with my gardens."

"Then you don't know you're our celebrity designer?"

Georgina thought of the word "Gob-smacked." She had never particularly liked it but now nothing else seemed appropriate. "I haven't done it for that." She faltered out an explanation. "I did it for me really, well for me and for all the little ones. We've all lost so much magic from our lives this year."

They rounded the corner and arrived back at the Dell. Girls and boys of all ages were still waiting their turn to investigate the snow grotto. Others had crept down the driveway to talk to the polar bear or examine the giant candy canes.

"We call you the Pied Piper." Sidney said stooping to examine the pixie ski slope.

Georgina was taken aback, "Oh I do hope not! My designs are built to mend not harm!"

She held the walking frame as Sidney took his time to straighten and regain his grip. "Perhaps then," he said slowly as he observed the enchanted face of a little girl with a pair of fairy wings pinned to her winter coat, "perhaps you would prefer Fairy Godmother?"

Their eyes met. Hers held the faintest flicker of amusement. They bumped elbows again. "Perhaps, I would" she said adding, "maybe you could inform *Community Face Book* of my name change?"

The End

Whatever I saw...

Whatever I saw you were not
the sun.
Whatever I hoped you were not
the moon.
Whatever I wished you were not
the stars.

Whatever you gave it was never
enough.
Whatever you took it was far
too much.
Whatever I heard it was not
a promise.

Whatever you said it was not
a truth.
Whatever was lost can never
be found.
Whatever they say you are
you are not...

Hope

Footnote: This was inspired by a poster with the breath-taking assertion across the middle: "I Am Hope."
Whether we put our trust in a person, a faith, a political party or ourselves; once again the Outlander suggests: History will be the judge.

Brevity of Life.
Light lost in a world's turn.
Tide and moon decide.

Love unrequited.
No chasing a setting sun.
This I have learned.

And far more besides.
Letting go takes more than time.
Memory lingers.

Haiku: Reflections on a life of learning

www.ingramcontent.com/pod-product-compliance
Lightning Source LLC
Chambersburg PA
CBHW061716130726
47996CB00006B/2340